Hi! We are the Whizz Writers.
Welcome to our book
'The Curse of the Nomed'
We are all students from
Four Dwellings Academy in Birmingham.

In 2018 we took part in the 'Look at our
Book' competition to create a story to be
turned into a book that will help pupils with
their move to secondary school.

left to right, Susan, Michaela, Jess (Coach) Joshua, Great, Farhaan

You cannot imagine how excited we were to
be crowned winners. We had so much fun
working as a team and creating the
characters that have been brought to life in
this book.

Being named as creators of our very own
book has just been epic!

We really hope you love our story as much
as we do, so get ready for an amazing
adventure! And we can't forget a big thank
you to our amazing coach Jess who has been
with us every step of the way!

First Published in Great Britain in 2018 by
Weird 'N' Wonderful Publishing

Curse of The Nomed
Idea created by the 'Whizz Writers'
of Four Dwellings Academy Birmingham
as part of the 'Look at our Book' Project by
Wesleyan to raise money for
Partnership For Children
Registered Charity number: 1089810
www.curseofthenomed.co.uk
with thanks to Wesleyan,
creators of the 'Look at our Book' project.

Written by BB Taylor Copyright © 2018 BB Taylor
Illustrated by Holly Bushnell
Copyright © 2018 Holly Bushnell
Curse of the Nomed Copyright © 2018 Wesleyan

A catalogue for this title is available from the
British Library
ISBN: 978-1-911146-13-1
First Edition

MIX
Paper from
responsible sources
FSC® C015395
FSC
www.fsc.org

Always look for adventure!

Best Wishes

BB

Curse
of the
Nomed

Dedicated to all the
adventurers out there.
Remember each new day
holds endless possibilities.

Chapter One

Sett straightened his tie and took one final look at his reflection in the mirror. Perfect. No-one would suspect a thing.

Until it was too late ...

The echoes from three pairs of footsteps raced at speed from different directions, shoes scraping and skidding as they drummed down the empty maze of corridors. As the three corridors joined, so did the three sets of feet, followed by three sets of eyes and the horror as they realised they were all too late.

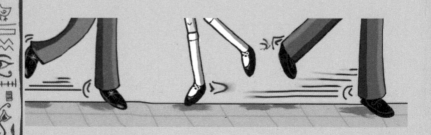

Recognising each other's faces and names from brief introductions before, the three of them felt a slight wave of relief; at least they weren't alone. But none of them wanted to speak first, in case they were overheard. In a whisper barely more than a hiss Eleanora spoke first.

'What are we going to do? We are sooooo done for!' Tears built up as she tried not to give in to them.

'Best bet we hide out til this is all over. It's the only choice I reckon,' Jacob replied, his eyes barely making contact with the other two as he ran his hands through his dark ruffled hair.

'I'm sure nobody will even notice. It's only assembly guys, not the end of the world!' sighed Stefan, wishing he was anywhere but there at that moment.

'But it's our induction assembly! And the letter from Inset Day clearly stated that we were not to be late. Under any circumstances. My Dad will be so angry if I get expelled on my first day.' Eleanora sniffled as she rummaged around in her pocket for a tissue.

'Look, Nora, all we have to do is lie low until it's over, then file in behind everyone as they come out. The old Headmaster won't even notice. I promise,' Stefan reassured her.

Eleanora nodded, not bothering to correct his lazy shortening of her name. Most people called her Nora anyway, except her Dad. Even her Mum had called her Nora, until she had passed away. Shaking herself off, she turned to Jacob who nodded in agreement. The three of them looked for the best place to hide until they could re-join their classmates.

Jacob, curious as to what they were missing out on, peeked his head up near the closest window. Not a sound could be heard from the room. It must have been soundproofed for music class, he thought as he watched carefully. All the new Year Seven students sat silently, eyes glued to the front of the hall and the figure smiling from the stage.

Mr S.Siriso, Headmaster of Nomed Academy stood, his arms raised wide, as a sinister look took over his previously charming face.

'Hey! Stef, Nora, you really need to see this. Something really weird is going on.' Jacob ushered them up to the window cautiously. Three pairs of eyes peeked through the window, feeling like they had been thrown into the middle of a scary movie.
As the Headmaster's lips moved, he raised his arms defiantly above his head, as his eyes began to glow!

All three gasped.

Nora, rubbing her eyes, blinked again to see if she was imagining the sight before her. Unfortunately she wasn't, and the madness did not end there. The eerie glow from their new Headmaster was matched by a similar glow coming from each and every one of the students. The entire hall looked like a freeze frame as each student sat silently; not moving, not blinking, just barely breathing. All were in time, not one out of sync.

Jacob located the source of the green glow from the students. 'Look! It's the badges. The badges are glowing!'

Nora and Stef watched on as the badges each student wore glowed vibrantly. The scarab beetle pin each of them had been sent with their uniform pulsated as the Headmaster continued his chant.

'Why aren't ours doing that? What is going on? This doesn't feel right.' Jacob looked down at his badge poking the dull lifeless beetle.

'Don't do that Jacob! You might set it off. We don't know what it's doing to them. Do you want to join them?' Stef snapped at his stupidity. No wonder everyone thought Jacob was a danger. Even Stef had heard the rumours about the fire.

'I think it's because we're out here. It's only the students inside. But why aren't the teachers doing anything? They must see what's going on. Why aren't they moving?' Nora whispered, not sure if she actually wanted to know the answer.

The three students reluctantly looked back inside the hall, looking for any sign that the teachers could see the strange goings on. But the teachers were just as transfixed as the students, even the Deputy Head, Miss Cleveland, seemed to be in the trance too. All eyes focused on the Headmaster, not one word seemed to escape from their lips. They all stood unnaturally still. All complete with their very own scarab beetle too.

Their eyes diverted from the statue-like teachers as the Headmaster gained their attention with a loud clap of his hands. Each felt their hearts pounding as the noise echoed, they realised the door was now open! Students all stood simultaneously and, with military like precision, they began to exit the hall, accompanied by their teachers.

Not waiting to find out what would happen next and no longer wanting to join the line, the three students did the only thing that felt right.

They ran.

Chapter Two

The door slammed behind them as they ran into the first empty room they found. They had moved as if their lives depended on it. Maybe they did?

This was not how the first day of school was meant to go.

You were meant to get lost. You were meant to feel nervous about making new friends. At no point did anyone mention the very strange Headmaster and mass army of zombie- like students.

Nora thought back to induction day at the Academy. It had been a very different picture to the one they had witnessed today. The students were loud and bubbly, and definitely not silent or still like they had just seen. And at no point did she recall seeing the Headmaster's eyes glow green when he welcomed them to Nomed Academy on their very first visit.

She had been so nervous about starting at the Academy. When she visited with her Dad to look round, it had seemed so big and creepy, but Headmaster Siriso had been so charming and kind, easing away any concerns she had about leaving her Dad behind. She worried so much about him being on his own since her Mum had died. The two of them had become so close since her death and she wasn't sure he'd even eat properly himself, let alone remember to feed the cat, but both her Dad and the Headmaster had supported and encouraged her and she didn't want to let either of them down.

Maybe the Headmaster was ill? Or possibly he had been replaced by an evil twin. You heard about it all the time on TV.

Confused, panicked and generally unsure what to do next, the three students looked around the room they had entered. Books were stacked from floor to ceiling with ladders propped up against the dark, old wood of the shelves.

'This must be the library. I don't remember visiting here when I came with my Dad to visit,' Nora said curiously as her fingertips brushed across the dusty tomes on the shelves.

'Doesn't look like anyone's visited here in a very long time. Either that or they need to sack the cleaner.' Stef sneezed as he opened a book, sending dust floating through the air.

None of them noticed the pair of eyes following them across the library. Studying them, watching them, deciding what exactly what to do with them.

Jacob looked around for another exit. There was only one way out - the door they had just come through. He didn't fancy seeing what awaited them out there. Just like Nora, he didn't remember seeing the library either, not that he had been paying attention. His mother had whisked them round the school, before signing him up as fast as she could. Anything to get him back on the straight and narrow.

No matter how many times he tried to say the fire was an accident, nobody believed him. He wasn't sure if he believed it himself anymore.

Loneliness had been his friend ever since. He knew that people would find out eventually and nobody would want to be friends with him. He was a danger to himself and those around him. Best option, stay quiet and try not to muck things up. A shiver trampled down his spine. He jumped, turning, but there was nothing there. Looking around he could see Nora and Stef exploring the library. But it felt like they were not alone.

'Hey, guys. Can you feel that?' he asked. Stef and Nora looked around confused.

'Feel what?' Stef replied.

'Nothing. Probably just me. I could have sworn we weren't alone.' Jacob's eyes continued to scan the room. Just like in the assembly something didn't feel right. But this felt different.

Stef ushered them over to a set of bookcases. 'Does anything look strange about these?'

They scanned the shelves looking for what he meant. Then it dawned on them. None of the books on those shelves were in English! In fact, most didn't even look like they had writing on them. They pulled out the nearest book to them, which was covered in pictures and symbols.

'That's Egyptian,' Jacob piped up. 'Looks like the pictures we saw in primary school when we learnt about Ancient Egypt.' He pointed to the pictures on the front, wrapped in gold outline, each looked delicately hand drawn.

'You're right! We did about them at our school too. My Dad helped me with a project all about the Pyramids.' Nora remembered all the glue and mess as she and her Dad tried to build their very own Pyramid for the class project. It was slightly wonky, but she was very proud of it. It still took pride of place in their living room. Her Dad had promised her they would go on an Egyptian adventure together one day.

CRASH!

They all jumped, fearful they had been discovered. It was only a matter of time before the Headmaster realised they were missing and came for them. Looking around they found the source of the noise.

Several books had fallen and standing next to them was the owner of the pair of eyes that had been watching them. Silently the four waited for someone to break the ice. Jacob jumped in.

'Who are you?'

'I'm Miss Ali, keeper of the books from the Great Library. And you three are not like the other students.'

Chapter Three

'So you're the Librarian?' Nora asked, still unsure whether they should be talking or running at this point.

'In a manner, I suppose I am. Yes.'

The Librarian's cryptic reply left the three students with a list of questions that was growing faster than the mould under Stefan's bed at home. She didn't look much like any Librarian they had ever seen. Her perfectly flawless dark skin shone, as her intricate makeup decorated her deep chocolate eyes. She looked more like one of the images from the books that littered the shelves of the neglected library itself.

'Please can you tell us what is going on? We are so confused. We didn't mean to be late for assembly, but then when we did get there it was all so strange and then we panicked and ran.' Nora began sniffling once more, her tissue still damp and crumpled from her earlier snot and tears.

'Speak for yourself! I wasn't panicked. I just followed you pair so you didn't get into more trouble.' Stef pushed out his chest, arms crossed. Another book fell with a dull thud, sending him running behind Jacob.

'Yeah, mate, really brave aren't you? Admit it, you were just as scared as we were and with every reason too. Did you see those glowing green eyes? That's not normal!' Jacob had no problem admitting he was terrified. Any sane person would be.

The Librarian stood and studied the trio. In all the millennia, she had never seen anyone escape the ritual. If he found out they had, he would be furious. She knew she was limited to what she could do, but she had waited long enough.

'I can't help you escape I'm afraid my young students. You see, I am trapped here in the library, as I have been for as long as I can remember. But I do want to help you,' she said sincerely. Her heart ached at the fear in the confused children before her.

'What do you mean you're trapped? The door is right there! You just walk right out of it, it's simple!' Stef pointed to the door. The poor woman was confused. He knew spending too much time round books was dangerous for your health, no matter what his parents said. Here was the proof.

The Librarian headed towards the door and reached for the handle.

As her hand made contact with the handle, a burst of light exploded from the door throwing her small figure across the room. Nora and Jacob raced to her side, checking she was all right as a shocked Stefan looked on. Okay, so maybe she wasn't lying.

'Are you okay Miss Ali?' Nora quivered as she tried to help the small woman to her feet.

'Yes I'm fine, child. What is your name?' she asked rubbing her throbbing back as she stood.

'I'm Nora, this is Jacob and that idiot over there is Stef.'

'Hey! How was I to know? You both think it sounds unbelievable too! I mean whatever next? Aliens and secret spies? This is school, not a video game.'

The Librarian scaled the ladder, scanning the shelves till she came to the book she was looking for. Carefully she slid the giant text off the shelf, balancing, as she wobbled back down the ladder. 'This may help to explain.' She opened the book on the nearest table wiping the dust from the pages.

'Many moons ago when the Gods were almighty and worshipped by all, there were two brothers, Sett and Osiris. Jealous of Osiris, Sett plotted to kill his brother and scatter the parts of his body so he couldn't be brought back to life, enabling him to take his place as ruler. But the plan didn't go as he had hoped. Sett was exiled as punishment, because their father loved them both and couldn't see any harm come to either of his sons. I was sent here to watch over Sett but he trapped me here in the House of Life- what you call the library- so I couldn't interfere in his plans to try and get revenge on his brother and father.'

19

The Librarian pointed to the scenes mapped out in the book, just as she described. Nora, Jacob and Stef were struggling to absorb what was going on. Their Headmaster wasn't a Headmaster after all. This just didn't happen. These were the sort of things that happened in movies or comics. Not on your first day of school. The Librarian turned the page of the book.

'Sett is weak. He doesn't have the strength to return yet. He is trying to collect power and build up his forces so he can return and launch his attack on them.'

The trio looked at each other, deciding whether they needed to pinch each other. Could they really believe this was going on? What were they going to do? They were ill-equipped to deal with homework and class timetables, how were they going to escape a power hungry teacher with a God complex? Jacob asked the question they were all thinking. 'So what does he want with us? We don't know anything about how to overthrow a God.'

The Librarian paused looking at the three innocent young students.

'He doesn't want your help Jacob. He wants your soul.'

Chapter Four

The room echoed with the chill of nothingness as the weight of those few words hit them. Their souls. The assembly wasn't just a welcome to Nomed Academy, it was a trap. One from which they were never meant to escape.

'The Assembly you missed, is where he puts everyone into a trance. Dark magic that should never be used on mortals. Once the trance is started, it buys him the time he needs to steal their souls. Trapping them here forever, slaves to Sett for all eternity. His strength is growing and with each soul he takes he is one step closer to returning.' The Librarian's eyes lowered unable to meet the students', the shame apparent in her face. The students looked down at their Scarab badges in horror, ripping them off as if they were on fire.

'So why haven't you done anything? You're supposed to be a Librarian, they read books and help people. They don't help evil ex-gods steal souls!' Stef stamped his foot, frustrated that Miss Ali could just do nothing.

'When we first arrived I tried to make him see sense. I begged and implored him in the name of the great God and his father Amun-Ra to seek forgiveness in his heart. But, his heart is black and his soul is poisoned with greed and jealousy that has only increased over time. When I tried to stop him he cursed me, trapping me here. I am doomed to guard the entrance to the inner vaults of the House of Life for all the lifetimes to come.' A single droplet rolled down her face, staining her flawless cheek as she looked around her prison.

'So you haven't even got a spare pair of clothes? No wonder your outfit looks so strange!' Stef pointed at the clothes she wore. They looked more like a fancy dress costume than an actual outfit. Jacob elbowed him in the ribs sharply, shutting him up before he upset the Librarian further. 'Shush you idiot, can't you see she's upset?'

Stef mumbled under his breath what sounded like an apology.

'The only way to stop him is the Book of Life. One of the Gods' most powerful spell books. But it's in the inner vaults and I can't get there.' The Librarian pointed to a bookcase. 'I was a Priestess in the House of Life, where all the magic books were kept and the spells were taught down through the generations. There is a passage way that leads down to it. It is only with that book that Sett can be stopped.'

'Well that shouldn't be too hard. We'll go and get the book for you, then you can mumble the magic words or wave your wand and we can go home and find a nice normal school with homework, detentions and dodgy school dinners,' Stef mocked jokingly. Nora and Jacob didn't share his enthusiasm.

'It is not that simple,' the Librarian replied regretfully.

'I had a feeling you were going to say that,' Nora sighed, deflated.

'The book you need is in the inner, deepest vault. There are traps and curses along the way, to stop the unworthy. The books are so powerful the Gods didn't want them falling into the wrong hands.' The trio looked at the Librarian. It didn't seem they wanted them in any hands by the sound of it.

'Let's look at our options here guys,' Stef interrupted. 'Do we really want to risk our lives trying to get a book that may not even exist? I think we should sneak out of the school and call the police. This has got to be a criminal matter. I mean stealing souls must be against the law, or at least be child neglect?'

'And what are you going to tell them Stef? *Hi Mr. Police Officer, our Headmaster is an evil Egyptian God who wants to steal our souls so he can get revenge on his brothers?* Yeah I'm sure they will be racing over here to help us! And, have you forgotten the fact we'd have to get back to the mainland first? This school isn't exactly easy to reach.' The sarcasm dripped from Jacob's lips as he smirked back at Stef.

The school was on a small island, just off the coast of Scotland. So small in fact that it didn't appear on any maps. The only way there was by boat and there was only a slim chance of getting away on one of them without being spotted by the Headmaster, or his mass army of students and teachers. It was the perfect place to hide an army of soulless students. Nora's stomach spun at the thought, sending her dizzy as she fumbled for a seat. There was no choice.

'Boys, I'm going after the book. Are you coming with me?'

They both looked stunned at her. She wasn't exactly superhero material. Little and quite fragile looking, Nora didn't really inspire confidence in the pair of them. But Nora knew at that point, if she ever wanted to see her Dad again, the quicker they got the book the better. She couldn't remember her Mum very well, but her Dad always told her stories of how pretty and funny she was. He didn't like talking about the accident, but he was more than happy to talk about Elle everyday so Nora never forgot her face. Clutching her locket she opened it looking at the picture inside, the last picture of all three of them, her very own treasure.

She stood, head high with a confidence that didn't really exist, as she looked at the Librarian.

'So how do we get this book?'

Chapter Five

The boys stared at Nora, debating whether she had lost her mind. It was only the first day of school and yet here she was, actually suggesting they consider this ridiculous plan. This wasn't a teacher with a grudge, or facing off with the school bully. This was an all-powerful Ancient God against three eleven year olds and a helpless Librarian. Jacob doubted it would be as simple as getting detention if they failed.

But what choice did they have?

The Librarian fumbled around the shelf, looking for something specific. Once she found the book she was looking for she gave it a tug. The floor rumbled as the shelves moved, revealing a door that hadn't been there before.

The large oak door looked as old as the library itself, encased in a stone frame engraved with lots of symbols and pictures. Jacob recognised them as hieroglyphs, just like the ones from primary school, but he couldn't understand what they said. Hieroglyphs were the ancient language of the Egyptians and each picture represented a different message or word.

Removing a rusty looking iron key from around her neck, Miss Ali twisted it in the lock waiting to hear the click as it opened for the students.

'This is as far as I can go. I cannot go beyond the door with you. Bring the book back to me and I can use it to stop Sett once and for all,' Miss Ali said, with a hope building in the depths of her heart that she hadn't felt in an eternity.

'Miss Ali, can I ask you something?' The question was burning Nora up and she needed to know the answer.

'Yes Nora?'

'If you are able to stop the Headmaster, why did he trap you here instead of just killing you?' Nora couldn't understand if the Headmaster was so evil, why he would spare her life in the first place.

'Because if I die, my soul will return to the Underworld where I will be able to warn Sett's brother Osiris. Sett has trapped me here, unable to escape or die to prevent me from doing so.'

Nora bowed her head, slightly ashamed for thinking so badly of the poor Librarian. What torture it must have been to be trapped alone for so long, with all hope gone. The trio looked at the open door, none of them wanting to step through but unsure what choice they really had. Darkness lay ahead with dangers they couldn't begin to imagine. Why hadn't they just picked a different school?

The boys held back letting Nora lead the way. So much for brave knights! Grabbing a torch from the wall she headed into the tunnel, which seemed to be leading down. The open flame from the torch flickered slightly, causing Jacob to freeze. His body locked in place. Memories flooded back to him of the fire, their home, their belongings. All gone and his poor brother injured. It was an accident, he kept telling himself. Nora, noticing the traumatised look on his face pulled the torch away from his gaze.

'You okay, Jacob?' He nodded, unable to talk but happy to be pulled from his thoughts, as they headed on further down into the tunnels.

The corridor continued down. They couldn't tell how far underground they actually were, but the yellow stone walls around them held no comfort as they felt more and more closed in. Stef, using his hands, felt his way along the walls, ensuring he didn't trip or fall. As his hand brushed past a bump in the wall, he realised his mistake. Jacob threw himself into the others pushing them to the floor as a stone wall came crashing to the floor behind them, blocking the way they had come. His body shaking from the adrenaline and shock, Jacob's legs gave way as he tried to stand. Stef and Nora pulled him to his feet.

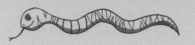

'Come on Jacob, we need to keep moving. I have a really bad feeling that was only the beginning.' Nora tried to coax him along but his body was in complete shock. Not knowing what else to do, Nora took her nails and pinched him on the ear as hard as she could. She was sure she had heard somewhere it was good for shock. As she had hoped, he jumped, pulling him back into focus.

'Are you with us, Jacob?'

He nodded to her, as Stef picked up the torch which was thankfully still lit. The trio continued on, wondering if they had made the right choice after all.

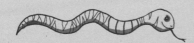
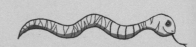

Keeping close to each other, but not wanting to actually touch each other, they cautiously continued on. A light ahead was becoming brighter. Hopeful that the book was just ahead, they perked up racing down towards the light and the opening ahead. As they left the corridor, they found themselves in a large room with a ceiling so high they couldn't see the top. Distracted by the new surroundings they failed to realise the entrance had closed behind them, or that the three of them seemed to be getting shorter, as the room got higher. As they felt a cold sludge around their ankles it became apparent what they had run into.

Quicksand!

They soon realised that false hope was a dangerous thing...

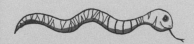
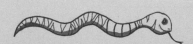

Chapter Six

Panic took over as they realised how quickly they were sinking and the quicker they sank the more they panicked. Ankles vanished, quickly followed by knees and the rest of them not far behind. All three began struggling to breathe as the realisation took over them that they were done for. Nora, desperately reaching her arms around, felt something solid.

The edge of the floor!

Closing her eyes and pulling herself with every ounce of strength she could muster, she heaved herself out over the edge of the sand pit. Refusing to open her eyes she sat, knees against her chest, back firmly against the wall, unable to breathe or concentrate, until the screams of the boys snapped her back into focus.

She needed to get them out, but how? With the exception of the quicksand, the room was empty and the boys were sinking fast, now chest deep with their arms in the air waving for her to help them. She could see the panic and desperation in their eyes, the same feeling she had encountered only moments ago herself.

But what could she do?

She wasn't a hero, she definitely wasn't brave, and quick thinking didn't come naturally either. Trying to calm herself so she could assess the situation and her options, Nora nervously twisted her tie in her hands, as she tried to find a solution. She couldn't help herself, she always did it when she was worried.

Her tie!

Taking the tie off, she undid it, tying a loop at the end. The loop was small enough for a hand to fit through. Stefan was closest but the tie wouldn't reach as far as Jacob. She needed to save both of them; they were in this together!

'Stef take your tie off. Quickly wrap it round both of your wrists,' she ordered. Stef and Jacob obeyed without question, hoping Nora knew what she was doing. Once she was sure the boys were connected she threw the looped end of the tie to Stefan.

He missed.

The quicksand was almost to their necks. She didn't have time to miss again. They wouldn't be able to breathe much longer. Taking a deep breath, she tried to steady her quivering hands as she took aim.

'You can do this Nora, just don't rush. We believe in you,' Jacob spoke calmly, trying to keep her calm too, even though inside, his brain was screaming in fear.

'We're right here with you Nora, you got yourself out, you will get us out too,' Stef added, trying to reassure the now shaking mess that was currently Eleanora. Swinging the soggy sand covered tie, she took one final breath.

The tie flew through the sky, landing ungracefully, smacking Stef straight in the face, quicksand and all.

But he had it!

Tightening it round his wrist as the sand now lapped at his chin, he nodded to Nora. She pulled as hard as she could, struggling to keep her feet steady under the slippery quicksand.

It was everywhere!

The sinking figures of the boys edged closer towards her. But she was still slipping closer and closer, back towards the edge.

She was going to fall back in!

Trying to keep pulling whilst walking backwards, she gave a steady pull, hoping the tie would hold. Stefan's hand grabbed onto the edge, pulling Jacob alongside. The pair sat side by side at the edge grinning, both looking like they'd won a gold medal, but both glad to feel the solid side, no longer sinking into the unknown depths of the quicksand.

Stefan gratefully handed Nora back her tie. 'Thanks Nora, just in time. Next time maybe we don't cut it so close?' He pulled off his sand-filled blazer, relieving himself of its excess weight.

'Next time! What do you mean next time! You both nearly died. We need to find a way out of here. Why on Earth did I think that we could do this? We've walked into a nightmare. I knew they said school could be scary on the first day, but I don't think this is what they meant,' Nora sobbed. She didn't want 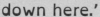 adventure. She was worried enough about making friends and not getting bullied without worrying about escaping from quicksand and ancient booby traps.

'I don't think that's an option anymore.' Jacob's face was solemn as he looked at his two companions. 'There's no way back. The only choice we have is to continue on and hope we can get through this. Together. We have each other, at least we are not alone down here.'

Nora and Stef nodded in agreement, Jacob was right. Three heads were better than one and at least they weren't completely alone.

They may have all been late for assembly, but at least now they knew the truth about what was going on. They could make a difference. Or at least try to. Discarding their blazers they tried to scrape as much quicksand off as they could, careful not to step too close to the edge again. It was always good not to repeat a decision that didn't have a positive outcome.

Surveying the room around them they saw the exit on the far side. Unsure how far the quicksand extended, they decided to stay as close to the walls possible. Using their ties, they stayed connected to each other, not quite wanting to hold hands but not wanting to lose each other again as they had so nearly done.

The path ahead was one they would take together.

Chapter Seven

Once more, they found themselves in a confined corridor, its sandy brick walls lined with lit torches and still descending further down.

'How far down do you think we are?' Nora asked the boys.

'I'd rather not know. Egyptian tombs went deep underground to keep the dead and their treasures safe. I'd rather not think about being in a tomb, if you don't mind. Tombs mean mummies.' Stef shuddered at the thought, remembering the pictures from their class project.

They had done a project all about how ancient Egyptians were embalmed and mummified, their brains pulled out through their nose with a hook and put in a jar to take to the afterlife. He heaved at the thought.

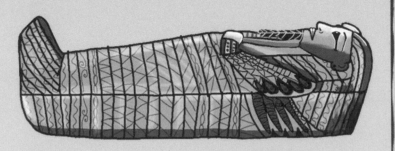

'You can't be serious. Mummies?' Nora giggled. But the stone-faced look from Stef suggested he wasn't joking.

'How can you joke Nora, after everything we've seen so far? It would be just our luck to run into something as crazy as a mummy,' Jacob replied, praying he was wrong. A torch flickered near Jacob's face. He jumped, unable to stop himself. He hated the flames, and how destructive and unpredictable they were. You just couldn't control them, he knew from experience. He could still feel the heat from the flames tingling against his face as if the fire was still there.

It haunted his dreams.

'Not keen on the fire then Jacob? I heard the rumours. From before school started. They say you were a bit of a fire fan,' Stef cautiously asked, curious to know the truth. Nobody knew the exact facts, but everyone had heard he had started the fire that injured his brother.

39

They were wrong. But who'd believe me. After all, teachers always told everyone I never listened and I didn't pay attention. So of course I was the bad kid. In the end, I stopped trying to tell them I wasn't,' Jacob sighed, his eyes still fixed on the flickering flame. 'When everyone tells you for so long that you're no good at anything, you give up trying. I did try my best at school before, honestly. I just needed a little help. But after the fire, nobody looked at me the same. I didn't start it, but there was no point trying to tell anyone that. They had already made up their mind.' Jacob waited for the accusing looks from his companions, but they never came.

'We believe you mate.' Stef placed a hand reassuringly on his shoulder and Nora nodded in agreement. 'New school, new start, Jacob. Well, it will be if we actually get out of here. But we believe you, and we will listen if you ever do want to talk about it.' Stef continued past him, leaving him to ponder what they had said. Nobody had ever asked him what really happened. His parents wouldn't talk about it and his brother didn't blame him but didn't stick up for him either, because then people would know the truth; that Jacob had done nothing wrong. But he didn't want his brother in trouble. He had suffered enough getting himself injured, he had learnt his lesson. But nobody up until this point had shown him such kindness.

Maybe this school wouldn't be so bad after all. If they survived.

Nora stopped dead in her tracks, Jacob and Stef bumping into her.

'What now?' she asked them. The trio stood faced with three paths but no clues which one led to the book.

'Don't any of these places come with simple directions?' Jacob huffed.

'What would you prefer? That one was labelled book this way and the other certain doom?' Stef smirked. Nora elbowed him, shushing him, as she listened for any clues.

'The book is probably going to be in the deepest part of this place, so we need to work out which path looks the steepest,' Nora said, hoping that was the logical solution. She didn't want to lead them into any more danger. They'd had enough for one day. She couldn't even tell how long they had been down there. It felt like days, but with no daylight or clocks it was impossible to tell. Her stomach began to growl. She couldn't remember the last time she ate.

'Was that a bear about to attack or your stomach, Nora?' Stef teased. Nora blushed, mumbling about feeling slightly hungry.
Jacob rummaged around in his pocket pulling out several snack bars, covered in quicksand, but still sealed. He shared them amongst the three of them. Quickly devouring the bars, the three of them soon realising how hungry they had been, distracted by the drama unfolding around them.

'Right, we need to decide which one to go down. I think we should vote,' Nora suggested looking for suggestions from the boys.

'The middle one looks like it has steps down so I think that one would probably go deeper, but we'd need to take a torch,' Stefan suggested. Jacob nodded not wanting to decide, he'd only get it wrong.

42

Nora removed a torch, and the three of them trekked into the darkness, one step at a time, none of them admitting that they were holding onto the ties connecting them just a little tighter than they had moments ago. Their stomachs whirled, but they ignored them, pushing on further down the staircase.

But they were not quick enough. As the staircase disappeared beneath their feet and all three of them went sliding down screaming uncontrollably, they wished they had listened to the warnings in their stomachs after all.

Chapter Eight

What was really only moments, felt like an eternity, as the three of them slid down into the darkness below. The empty abyss welcomed them at an increasing speed. The echoes of their screams piercing each other's ears as they crash landed on top of each other, with poor Nora squashed under weight of the two boys, who landed awkwardly, still all attached by their ties.

The torch rolled across the room, thankfully still lit, shedding light on their destination as they untangled themselves from a blushing Nora. They released the ties, not wanting to repeat the experience again. Dusting themselves off, they tried to work out the best direction to head in.

'Wait!' Nora snapped. 'Don't move a muscle.'

The boys, who were already tired and scared, looked bewildered as they tried to work out why she was so snappy. Their eyes glanced down. The floor below their feet was divided into squares all different sizes and heights, each with a picture on top. It was a booby trap and they had landed straight on it.

'Anyone fluent in hieroglyphs?' Stef nervously chuckled, his eyes darting from stone to stone.

'Yeah mate, just give me a second and I'll get out my handbook!' Jacob replied with an unimpressed smirk.

'Will you pair stop it! Stop talking, stop moving, stop arguing! I'd say stop breathing too if I thought it would shut you both up!' Nora's breathing was becoming tighter. All she needed was these two arguing on top of everything that was going on. They were just three normal students, all from very different backgrounds and different places. But essentially, they were all just three frightened students who had hoped for a slightly different start to the school year.

The boys, both looking ashamed, eyes not making contact, spoke at the same time. 'Sorry Nora,' they said. She nodded back to them, trying to stay as still as she could while they tried to muddle their way through the room. Her foot started to tighten, the muscles under the arch of her foot seizing up as she desperately tried to stay still.

'I've got cramp in my foot! I don't know what to do!'

The colour ran from Stefan's and Jacob's faces. Jacob tried reassuring her. 'Try not thinking about it. Try focusing on something else, anything! Just don't think about it!'

Nora bit the inside of her cheek as hard as she could. She could taste the blood trickling inside her mouth. It was working! The cramp started to fade, as relief washed across her face.

'ACHOOO!' Stefan's hands reached for his face automatically, his whole body shifting slightly as the sneeze escaped.

Too late.

Nora had been right, the floor was a trap. Stefan's sneeze set in motion a series of moving stones beneath their feet. The three of them froze. Not sure whether to run, or try and stay still and wish for the best. None of them could react quickly enough though, as the floor swallowed them up.

They all tumbled down the hidden traps in the floor, nothing but darkness surrounding them. Their worst fears were realised as they fell.

They were alone.

Each of the trio had worried about the loneliness of starting a new school, but this wasn't what they had imagined. No noise or light - just the whistling and endless falling. Taking them deeper than they had ever been before, unsure if they would fall for eternity, feeling lost and scared.

But their destination did come.

Three separate landings. One with a splash, one with a thud and one with a rustle. All followed by the heavy impact of metal around them.

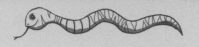

Nora tried to stand, unable to move forwards or backwards because of the cage around her. Both of her shoes now filled with the sand she had landed on with a dull thud. Pouring the sand out of her shoes, she looked at the cage that trapped her, noticing two more on opposite sides of the triangular room. Both with occupants.

Jacob had landed with a splash into a deep filled well also surrounded by a cage, neatly wrapped around its rim, leaving him no way to pull himself out. He tilted his head back trying to remember those swimming lessons his mother had forced him and his brother to go to in case they ever got stranded at sea. He had laughed at the time ...

Stefan, still looking at his two classmates, neglected to notice the rustling in his cage as he rubbed his back, aching from the landing. He seemed to have landed in the safest of the three cages. Or so he thought, until a slither under his trouser leg caused him to squeal.

Snakes. And lots of them.

Stefan closed his eyes, trying to focus on his breathing, hoping in desperation that none of them were venomous, or hungry.

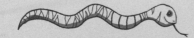
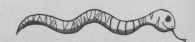

There were no doors, no locks, no keys. Just a large chain above each of the cages, and three levers in the walls behind them. They were much too heavy for any of them to lift, even if one of them could escape to free the others. It would take something very big or very strong to be able to release them.

The floor shook, like an earthquake. It shook again, almost like steps coming towards them getting louder as the rumbling got heavier. As a door lifted, it released exactly what it was that was strong enough to lift those cages. Nora wasn't sure if they were safer in or out of the cage, as the fourth figure entered the room.

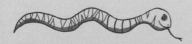
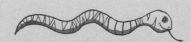

Four gigantic paws, resembling those of a lion, only much bigger, were followed by a gigantic body, which crouched slighly to fit through the door into the chamber, and attached to it was the head of a man, with a stern face and eyes that seemed to look into your soul. It addressed them in a very gentle, yet terrifying voice.

'Who dares to enter the chamber of the Sphinx?'

Chapter Nine

None of them dared to speak, unable to believe what they were seeing before their eyes. A real life Sphinx! They had seen pictures and read about them in primary school, but not one of them believed the stories to be anything more than a legend - like Santa Claus or the Tooth Fairy. It stalked the three cages, just as a lion would before eating its prey. Stefan secretly hoped it had already had a decent lunch. It turned on Nora, eyes firmly locked her hers.

'Tell me your name,' it demanded.

Quivering, she whispered, 'Nora' not daring to make eye contact with the terrifying creature. It paused before replying with a booming voice, 'That is not your name! What is your true name?' The boys looked on confused, concerned for Nora but also fearful for themselves as well. It roared once more, 'I will not ask again, answer me or be devoured. What is your true name?'

'Eleanora Dorothy Annabelle Williams,' she blurted out, praying it was the right answer. She didn't know what it meant. It was the only name she had. But the Sphinx nodded continuing on to the next cage. Stefan's.

Again it asked, 'Tell me your name.' With a lump stuck in his throat he replied too, aware of the hissing still twisting round his feet. 'Stefan Nathaniel Madden.' It nodded turning its attention to the last cage. Jacob. Jacob's legs were now becoming tired from treading water. He clung to the bars around the well, his fingers cold and sore. His arms were beginning to ache as well.

'Tell me your name,' it asked for the third time.

Jacob's tired voice replied, 'Jacob Fergus Blossom,' too worn out to care if anyone laughed. He always begged his teachers when he was younger not to use his full name, but they never listened. He was past the point of worrying about what other people thought of his stupid name. His mother had always said it was a name to be proud of, but he wasn't so sure he had anything to be proud of at the moment except his survival swimming badge, and even then, he knew he couldn't hold on much longer.

52

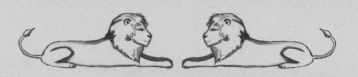

'Three intruders in my home,' the Sphinx said, speaking softly once more. 'No doubt thieves trying to rob the treasures I have been set to guard?'

'No!' protested Nora. 'We are not thieves, the High Priestess, Miss Ali, sent us to retrieve the Book of Life. She is trapped by Sett. He has taken over our school.'

'LIES!' The Sphinx silenced them with the painfully loud reply. Many had tried to steal its treasures over the passing of time. None had succeeded so far.

'Why would we come all the way down here and risk our lives, if it wasn't important?' Jacob mumbled trying not to swallow the water lapping around him.

Nora tried to reason with the creature. 'She told us that with the Book of Life the Egyptian God, Sett, could be stopped, and that he had trapped her rather than killing her, so she couldn't return to the Underworld to warn Osiris that Sett is using an amulet to steal souls and build his strength.'

53

The Sphinx paced around the chamber, judging and watching the three trying to decide what to do. Eventually it stopped in the centre of the room. 'If you three intruders are sent by my High Priestess, then you are meant to have the book.'

The three of them sighed with relief. Finally something was going to plan.

'However, you will each have to answer a riddle first to prove you are worthy'

The relief was swiftly flooded with panic.

Stefan asked what they were all thinking.

'What happens if we get any of the riddles wrong?'

The Sphinx flashed its claws as it smiled. 'I will devour you all of course.'

Nora's face paled, her legs giving way as she stumbled to the floor of her cage.

The Sphinx continued. 'You entered as a three, so must you leave as a three, or stay as a three course meal. You will have three guesses each, no more, and you shall answer your own question, without help from your companions. Try to cheat me and you will all fail. Do you understand?'

54

The trio glanced at each other before nodding, their voices not co-operating or responding as they drank in the peril they were in. There didn't seem to be too many other options available. At least if they stalled for time, thought Nora, maybe another solution would present itself. Stef spoke up again. 'How do we know you won't just devour us anyway even if we get it right?'

The thought had crossed Nora and Jacob's minds too.

There was no way of knowing if the creature had the book, let alone if would let them go even if they got all three riddles right. But again, they realised their options were limited and Jacob was getting weaker by the moment, the coldness setting in and his arms becoming heavier as the cold water weighed him down.

'YOU DARE TO QUESTION MY HONOUR?'

Stefan immediately regretted voicing the question as the enraged beast rounded on him. 'I am the almighty Sphinx, entrusted by the Gods as guardian to the Book of Life and Death. I exist to serve. There will be no more wasting time, no more insults from you three intruders. If you wish to live, it is answers you must give.'

All three occupants of the cages looked to each other for reassurance. They had got this far, thought Stefan, how hard could a few riddles really be? Maybe they would be simple. They were from ancient times after all and people weren't as clever back then .... Were they? Nora, on the other hand, could feel the anxiety setting in, like a weight pressing her chest, her head throbbing and her legs still feeling unsteady. She was terrible at thinking on her feet, and she wasn't naturally clever. This was not going to end well at all. Jacob just wanted it to be over. He was beginning to need the loo, surrounded by all that water.

The Sphinx began.

Chapter Ten

As if the Sphinx could smell weakness, it rounded in on Nora first. Prowling towards her, she let a nervous squeak escape her lips, closing her eyes as it approached her prison.

'Eleanora Dorothy Annabelle Williams. What is the creature that walks on four legs in the morning, two legs at noon and three in the evening?'

Nora wanted the floor to open back up and swallow her whole. There was no way she was going to get this. She didn't even understand what it meant! Nora remembered how hard she had struggled at school when they had covered Egypt and the Sphinx was one of the things that confused her the most. How could such a terrifying beast be made of so many different creatures yet still talk like a normal everyday man?

Then it hit her!

They had done this very riddle in class. Taking a deep breath she looked at the Sphinx sounding more confident than she felt as her body shook from the nerves. 'It is man, I think, well a person, I mean. When they are a baby they crawl, as an adult they walk and as you get older, you use a stick to support you.' She averted her eyes from the Sphinx waiting to be devoured by the hungry beast.

'Correct.'

Astonishment flooded across her face as she felt a weight lifted from her shoulders. She hadn't failed! The boys nodded reassuringly across to her with a mix of relief and worry. They both knew it was all on them now. Stefan was next. Still trying not to move, or anger the snakes still actively dancing around him, he tried instead to focus on the terrifying creature in front of him.

'Stefan Nathaniel Madden. What is always coming but never arrives?'

Stefan froze in panic. He didn't understand the riddle at all. He played the words over and over in his head, completely blank. His mind couldn't even guess an answer. Not even a clue as to what it could be. All he could think of was being eaten alive by the beast. The Sphinx interrupted.

'Your first answer?'

Stefan knew he wouldn't wait forever and said the only thing that came to mind.

'A ghost?' he guessed awkwardly.

'Incorrect. You have two guesses left and I will not wait all day for them.'

Stefan sighed. He had panicked and rushed. He didn't understand, it wasn't like the Sphinx had anywhere else to be today, or tomorrow or even the next day. So what was the rush?

Wait - that was it!

He knew the answer. Or at least he hoped he did. He replayed the answer over again in his head. It had to be right! Apprehensively, he spoke again.

'Tomorrow?'

'Correct.'

Relief filled his face for a spilt second, until he realised what he was still surrounded by, as a cold scale made contact with his leg. He had never been scared of snakes before, but he had never been locked in a cage with them before either. Gritting his teeth, he closed his eyes, waiting for it to pass before breathing again. The Sphinx had already moved on.

Last question.

'Jacob Fergus Blossom, last of the three intruders to my chamber. For you and your companions to leave here, you are their only hope. Only three chances you will have, or you will all be devoured.'

Jacob nodded, saving his breath. There was no point trying to beg or plead with the creature. He could see in its eyes - it only had one focus - protecting its treasure from anyone it deemed unworthy. But Jacob hadn't been worthy of anything in his life. His family didn't believe in him, so why would anyone else?

His mind flicked back to his earlier conversation with Nora and Stef.

They had believed him.

And now they needed him, he wasn't going to let them down.

'Jacob Fergus Blossom, I am an instrument that you can hear, but you cannot touch or see me. What am I?'

They were all doomed.

Jacob thought instantly, he had never played an instrument, he couldn't even read music. But maybe it wasn't a real instrument? Riddles were meant to be tricky weren't they and to confuse you. So what could make a noise a bit like an instrument that you couldn't see or touch. He had it! He knew the answer, they were free.

'The wind. It's the wind, it whistles, but you can't see or touch it,' he said proudly, finally accomplishing something important and saving the day.

'Incorrect.'

The world froze, shattering around him. No! It had to be right it was the only thing that made sense. It was the logical choice. The only other thing you can't see are well ...

'Is it a fart?' It slipped out from his tongue. He was unsure of himself after being so sure the first time, so he had said the first thing that came to mind, immediately realising that he had said it out loud and how very wrong it was.

'Incorrect. One answer left Jacob Fergus Blossom.'

What little strength he had left, drained out of him as his fingers slipped from the bars releasing him into the water. The cold unforgiving liquid filled his mouth as he sank down into the darkness. Realising he was alone and falling he tried to scream for help, but his voice wouldn't work.

His voice!

Giving it everything he had left, he kicked his way back up towards the light, gasping for air as his head bobbed up above the water. Nora and Stefan gasped too, thinking they'd lost him, hearts fighting to escape through their chests as their stomachs twisted with worry for both him and themselves. Gasping for air he tried to speak, but the words were jumbled until he finally managed one clear word.

'VOICE!'

He realised his voice was an instrument. The only one you couldn't see or touch. Jacob secretly loved to sing, but was embarrassed, so had never shared his secret with anyone. Not a single soul. But yet, his voice was the one thing he truly liked about himself.
Interrupted by his thoughts the Sphinx spoke. The three of them held their breath once more in nervous anticipation, as it spoke. Everything hung on this one answer, their fates were intertwined.

'CORRECT.'

Chapter Eleven

All three of them waited in dreaded silence to see if the beast was true to his word, or if they were destined to be on the menu for today. None of them knew if they could trust the beast before them but there was no escape if he was hungry.

The Sphinx turned its back on Jacob, its giant paw pulling the lever down, raising the cage over his watery prison. Again it did the same with Nora's and Stefan's. Nora raced to Jacob, helping to pull him out, followed closely by Stefan who was shaking his legs uncontrollably, unsure whether any snakes had tried to hitch a free lift. Standing together as close as they could, no longer worried about if they were too close, they waited.

Not as three students, or a team thrown together, they stood as a group of friends, willing to help each other to find a way through. No matter how scary the path was, they had each other. They believed in each other.

They just hoped they weren't lunch together.

Without a word, the Sphinx turned, returning from where it came. Jacob followed first, closely followed by the other two; it was the only exit from the chamber and they all wanted out of there as fast as possible. It led them into an adjoining room, so bright they had to shield their eyes when they first entered.

It was filled with jewels and treasures as far as the eye could see, a vast brightness shining across the room. In the middle stood two stands, each with a dull looking book perched on it closed.

'Do not touch anything except the item you seek,' the Sphinx warned as they entered the room. But the students struggled to focus on the dull boring book when there were so many amazing and beautiful treasures around them. They had never seen such riches and treasures. It was like they had stumbled into Aladdin's cave.

65

Crowns of gold dressed in rubies and emeralds. Swords with gems imbedded into the handles. Piles and piles of gold everywhere - so much it would take a lifetime to count. There was no way anyone could need so much. None of them were rich and none of their families were well off. Surely a tiny bit wouldn't be missed?

A tiny voice in each of their heads spoke to them, guiding them along, whispering, tempting, enticing them. Just one jewel, just a few coins. It could change your life and nobody would ever know, the whisper told them. But Jacob knew the truth.

He would know.

Snapping himself out of whatever trance he was in, his eyes searched for Nora and Stef, both still dazed and floating along, probably hearing the same voices he had heard too. Racing to them as their hands reached out towards the jewels, he grabbed them back.

'No. Don't be tempted. The Sphinx was very clear.'

Jacob glanced at the Sphinx, sitting at the other end next to the books, waiting to see what choice they made. It was another test. Nora and Stef, both realising what they had almost done, looked horrified, staring at their hands. It had been like someone else was driving their bodies, controlling their choices and moves. Jacob ushered them on.

'Come on. The book is just ahead, not much further now.'

Approaching the stands, they looked at the two books side by side. They both looked very similar. Nora looked at them, careful not to touch. 'But which one is the Book of Life?'

The Sphinx replied, 'Only take the item you came for.'

But how did they know which book it was? None of them read Egyptian! Stefan stared at the two books, but there was no way to tell.

67

'We're going to have to guess, I think this one on the right.' The other two nodded, there was no choice. None of them could read it and the Sphinx wasn't offering up much help either.

Stefan reached towards the book on the right, when Nora suddenly smacked his hand away.

'Ouch what was that for?' he complained, nursing the stinging hand.

'Just look, the one on the right and the left both have a figure on them. The one on the right has the head of a black animal like a dog thing. The one on the left is holding the sun. I think the one of the right is Anubis.'

Jacob interrupted. 'Wasn't he something to do with death?'

Nora nodded. 'Yes he guided the dead, so surely he wouldn't be on the cover of the Book of Life, would he?'

All staring at each other, they nodded again, this time all reaching for the same book.

The one on the left. The Sphinx rose to its feet.

'You have chosen your item. You must now leave this place, or be trapped here forever.' It gestured to a door behind it, which was similar to the very first one they had entered in the library. They sighed.

Now for the long trek back with the book.

But would they be able to keep it safe through whatever traps or danger lay ahead? thought Jacob. Looking down at his soggy tattered uniform, he hoped the book was a bit more durable than his clothes were.

'But how do we know we've got the right book?' Nora asked, worry eating away at her. Had she made the right decision?

'We don't,' Stefan replied his shoulders slumping as he too worried about the choice they had made.

'So this could all be for nothing?' The despair was clear in her strained voice.

'Better hope not, I'm all out of breakfast bars and I really need the loo. I'm not going back through all that again,' Jacob replied to them both bluntly, hoping they had made the right choice.

There was only one way to find out.

As they approached the door, they turned, listening to the Sphinx speak once more. 'The power of you three is not about magic or strength. It is about the choices that you make. Follow the wise choices and they will always lead you down the right path. Good luck my three intruders and farewell.'

Grabbing the door handle, with Stef behind him holding the book tightly and Nora looking nervously by his side, Jacob twisted the handle taking an apprehensive breath as he opened the old battered door.

The three of them were ready to face the unknown waiting for them on the other side.

Chapter Twelve

As they opened the door, none of them were prepared for what they found.

The library!

They were back in the library. In school. No more traps, no more running and most importantly, no more needing the loo! All three of them grinned at each other from ear to ear bouncing from foot to foot excitedly. They were finally safe! They hugged each other tightly with relief before jumping back realising they weren't alone.

A worried looking Miss Ali hurried to her feet. She had prayed to every God she knew, hoping they had heard her plea to keep the children safe and get them through. No person should have to go through what they must have endured, let alone three students.

'My young students! Thank the beautiful Goddess Isis you are all safe! Did you get the book? Did you succeed?'

Stefan handed her the battered looking book.

'We hope we got the right one, because not to be rude Miss, we really don't want to do that again.'

The Librarian gently took the book from him, staring at it like a lost treasure was in her hands. Looking over the book she gave them a reassuring nod confirming it was indeed the one they needed. Opening it up on a nearby table, she spoke quickly.

'We need to work quickly. The Headmaster will soon have worked out that he is missing three students and he will come looking for you. We cannot afford to waste time. This could be our only opportunity.'

She began moving a dusty old rug that took up most of the library floor. Without a word, Jacob began helping her to roll it out of the way, whilst Stefan and Nora cleared the floor of the scattered furniture to give her space for whatever she needed to do.

Miss Ali began carving out complex patterns and hieroglyphs inside the large triangle she had drawn, as she followed what they presumed to be instructions in the book. Stopping she looked up at them, with a focus in her eyes they had not previously noticed.

'I will create a spell that will turn my amulet into a prison, just like the one he uses. Except mine won't just trap his soul, but his body too. Then, I can return him to the Underworld where his brother Osiris can throw the amulet into the fires of the Underworld, trapping him forever for his crimes. Once the spell is complete, we will lure him here so I can trap him.'

Stef's head snapped up at her last lingering sentence. 'When you said we, you mean us. Don't you?'

She slowly nodded, regret clear in her eyes. 'I need him to be close enough to say the chant and trap him, but as you know I cannot leave. I have asked so much from the three of you already. But it is the only way I can save you. All of you. I will need your help to balance the spell, so we can complete it quicker. Normally the High Priests and Priestess would help.'

Once the triangle was complete, she gestured for the three of them to sit at each of the three points of the shape, as she sat in the middle, amulet cupped neatly in her hands. Unlike the Headmaster's, this wasn't a beetle of a badge, it more resembled a key of sorts, and as she chanted it turned a deep, velvet purple rather than the eerie green, with gold inscriptions glowing across it as she continued to chant. Unsure what they were meant to do, they sat still as instructed, eyes transfixed on the Librarian as she beautifully chanted. Her angelic voice weaving the spell to seal him in her amulet and free them once and for all.

A sharp gush of wind swept from each corner of the room, heading directly towards her. She quickly held up the amulet, sucking the wind into the object with the glow pulsing slightly before turning dull, the inscription now invisible.

'It is done. All we need now is the Headmaster.'

Nora looked around the library warily. 'Isn't he going to notice when he walks in if he sees the inscriptions on the floor and the room looking rearranged? Won't he suspect something is going on?'

Miss Ali and the boys nodded in agreement. Placing the amulet in her pocket, she and the students set to work, removing all traces of their actions. None of them wanting to waste the effort they had been through or only chance they would have.

They made quick work of removing the inscriptions from the floor and putting the furniture back as closely to its original positions as they could remember. They were nearly done. Then the scary part would start for the three nervous students. Luring the Headmaster back to the library, without getting caught or losing their souls. It sounded simple. But Nora felt sick just thinking about it and the boys didn't look overjoyed at the thought either.

They had come this far though.

With just the rug left to put back Miss Ali began rolling it back out, slowly tiptoeing backwards across the clear floor, where the enchantment had been previously inscribed. She smiled as she stood up, hands in her pockets looking across the library. Such brave students before her, who had accomplished so much in the face of such a great challenge and her, soon to be finally free, able to feel the sun on her face and its rays on her neck.

She could almost feel the breeze against her neck.

But there was no breeze in the library. Her body froze, paralysed in fear - a sudden realisation dawning across her mind. She rapidly pulled her hands out of her pockets, dropping the amulet before she had chance to use it.

'Hello Miss Ali. I've come to check out a book.'

Chapter Thirteen

There was no need to turn around. She could recognise that voice in any world. She tried to stall for time so she could get to the amulet without him noticing.

'Headmaster, how lovely to see you. It's so rare that we get a visit from you. What kind of book were you looking for? Maths, Science, maybe Astronomy?'

'Do not play with me Priestess. I am the God of Storms and the son of Amun-Ra. I do not take kindly to games,' he threatened, no kindness or mercy in his voice.

The three students froze, hoping by some miracle he wouldn't notice them while his attention was on the poor Librarian he now had gripped by her arm. But they did not go undetected and luck definitely wasn't on their side.

'Ah, our newest students. I believe you missed assembly, tut tut, but fear not. I have the whole school assembled especially for you. Can't have you missing out now can we? Especially after you brought me the one thing I was missing to complete my journey home. The book.'

He gestured to the door, clicking the fingers on his free hand. Several teachers appeared, taking the book, and escorting the trio toward the door. Forcefully. Nora tripped over the carpet by Miss Ali's feet, the boys stopping to help her back up. She smiled at them gratefully, apologising with tears freely streaming down her soft cheeks as they were ushered on out of the door past her, back towards the hall, where it had all started. Sett turned the Librarian to face him with a gleam in his eyes.

'You don't get out of this library enough Miss Ali, why don't you join us for assembly? It's sure to be unforgettable.'

He pulled her out through the barrier, which had entrapped her in the library, dragging her towards the hall, where everyone was waiting silently. She passed row upon row of soulless figures all trapped under his command, young and old. Teachers and students alike, and she had failed them all. But, at least they weren't aware of what was going on, unlike the three frightened students being held on the stage ahead. They knew exactly what was going on and the fear in their eyes told her just how much she had failed them too.

Once up on stage the doors slammed around the room, one by one. Followed by the terrifying click of each one locking. They were trapped. Nora looked across the sea of blank faces. Her class-mates. She barely knew them, but each one was a person just like her, nervous about starting school, excited about making new friends. None of them had seen this coming and none of them had even had a chance to escape.

But they did. The four of them. They had the chance to stop him and they had failed. If only they had worked harder, or faster. Maybe this wouldn't have happened. A salty droplet rolled down her cheek as she realised she'd never see her Dad, or her cat Naveen, ever again. She closed her eyes, picturing their faces as the fear took control and her heart raced uncontrollably.

Stefan wondered if his family would even notice he was gone. They didn't seem to notice him much at home. He had been so excited about starting school, a chance to make friends, to be noticed. This wasn't the kind of attention he'd had in mind though.

Jacob knew nobody would miss him. They could barely look him in the eye at home, still blaming him. At least he was here with two people who believed in him and helped him. Even if he did still need the loo.

The Headmaster beckoned for the book to be brought up. Miss Cleveland, the Deputy Headmistress, slowly ascended the stairs compliantly, carrying the book towards the Egyptian God as he triumphantly basked in the glory of his victory.

'And now, all I need is one more soul to complete my journey home, but which should it be? A student? One of you three?'

He pointed at each of them one by one, as their stomachs spun and their legs quivered in fear struggling to keep themselves upright.

'No, I'm afraid you just won't do, we need something special for our last one, something like ... a High Priestess maybe?'

Miss Ali's face paled as she realised just why he had kept her trapped in the library for so long. Not only did he need the book, but her soul too. She had played right into his hands and given him what he wanted.

It was all her fault.

'Now now, Priestess, why so glum? You are free of the library. I always knew you would find a way to get the book, you just didn't realise it was for me. You couldn't stand to see the poor students suffer. I knew that eventually you would find a way.'

She crumpled, broken and filled with despair as two of the teachers propped her up, ready for Sett to begin. His grin stretched from ear to ear.

'It will all be over soon, and then I can go home. Oh I do love a good family reunion.'

He began to chant. Just as he had done in the first assembly. Nora, Stef and Jacob tried to struggle free, but it was no use. The teachers restraining them were too strong. They watched in horror as Sett reached out, touching her face as he completed the chant, Miss Ali no longer struggling, empty.

The green glow faded, locking her soul inside the amulet. Nora felt her heart crack. No - she couldn't be gone. She was going to save them. She was going to fix it all and keep them safe.

Who would protect them now?

Chapter Fourteen

The Headmaster rounded on the students, enjoying the fear leeching from them. He could almost smell it like a tasty snack. He didn't need any more souls, but just because he didn't need them didn't mean he wasn't going to take them anyway. Power was just like a good meal. But once you've eaten at your favourite restaurant, you're left wanting more and more.

Sett had found his appetite to be relentless. No matter how many souls he took, no matter how much power he had, it would never be enough. He wanted more. He turned looking at the tasty snacks in front of him as they simmered away, cooking in fear.

'So children, who wants to get extra credit and go first?'

Stef struggled trying to get free, looking for a possible escape. 'You said you didn't need us, why are you doing this?'

why, because I can of course,' Sett chuckled. The confidence just radiated off him. It may have taken an eternity but he had won. And this victory meal would be as sweet as any dessert.

'I'll go first,' the voice quivered. 'I don't want to be the last on my own.' Nora was released by the arms holding her as she stepped forward.

'That's both very brave and very cowardly at the same time, Eleanora isn't it? I remember you from induction day. Is school everything you hoped it would be?' he asked with a smile.

'Just get on with it,' she demanded. 'Please.' Her voice faltered, aware of what she was about to become. But at least she wouldn't be afraid anymore, no matter what happened she wouldn't be afraid.

'As you wish, my dear.' He bowed mockingly before beginning the chant.

His eyes glowed, as he reached out towards her, she no longer had her beetle, so he had to make contact. His arm almost in touching distance, she could feel a pull. It would all be over soon.

As the Headmaster was about to make contact, Nora took a deep breath ready.

It was now or never.

She shoved the Librarian's amulet into his open hand.

He screamed as though he was being ripped into a thousand pieces. The amulet in Nora's hand shone brightly, just as it had done in the library. Stefan and Jacob looked on, stunned at the sight before them. They hadn't even noticed Nora pick up the amulet.

They both realised, she must had grabbed it when she fell in the library!

Nora had hoped she could get the amulet back to Miss Ali so she could perform the ritual to save them. But with Miss Ali soulless all hope was gone, Nora had to try. She was unsure what exactly would happen.

But something was definitely happening.

The Headmaster tried desperately to escape the amulet's pull, but it was no use. His own power had cast the chant, his own power was pulling him in and there was nobody more powerful than him.

He was finished.

Stef, Nora and Jacob looked on as he was pulled into the amulet, arm first, then the rest of him following. It was horrific to watch as his body twisted and contorted but none of them could look away, no matter how much they wanted to. They had to make sure he was gone. With one last scream of despair, the amulet locked him in, sealing itself, the glow disappearing. Only one thing survived.

His amulet.

Nora stood, one amulet in each hand, transfixed. She jumped as she felt a hand on her shoulder.

Jacob.

They looked around the hall, for a sign of movement. But there wasn't even a blink. Every student, every teacher, even Miss Ali was frozen. Stefan wasn't even sure if they were still breathing.

'So what do we do now?' Stefan asked as he waved a hand in front of Miss Cleveland, hoping for some sign of life.

'I'm not sure, but we can't leave them like this. They'll starve to death!'

'How will they go the loo?' Jacob asked still thinking of his own bladder.

As they examined the beetle amulet, they looked for a button or a switch to reverse the process, but there was nothing and the book gave no answers either as they flicked through it, still in their teacher's hands.

There was no hope.

They had stopped Sett, but failed to save everyone else. How would they explain this to anyone? What if Ofsted turned up for inspection? Jacob took the beetle amulet from Nora, rolling it around in his hands. The souls of everyone in the hall were in the palm of his hands, and goodness knows who else was trapped in there too? How did they all fit in there? Jacob stared at the amulet thinking about how cramped it must feel - all those poor souls, trapped in there, just wanting to break out. Like keeping an animal in a tiny cage for the rest of its life. They couldn't just leave them there.

Carefully he set the amulet down on the floor, looking at his two companions. They looked curiously at him, unsure of what he was going to do.

Taking a deep breath, Jacob jumped on the amulet with all the force he could manage, smashing its emerald green wings. The amulet shattered underneath the weight of his still soggy school shoes. An explosion of light burst from the cracks, blinding the three of them.

Well it had definitely done something, the question was what?

Chapter Fifteen

Struggling to see anything, Stefan, Nora and Jacob covered their eyes as tightly as they could. The pain from the light was unbearable. As the light subsided, they cautiously peeked through the cracks in their fingers.

Everyone was still. It hadn't worked.

Feeling defeated, Jacob's shoulders slumped, weighed down by the guilt of what he had done. He had broken the amulet and trapped everyone forever. All thanks to him.

'You can't blame yourself you know, Jacob.' Nora sat down next to him as she tried to reassure him. They had done more than most students would have managed on their first day of school.

'Most people get lost on their first day or lose their bag. We defeated an Egyptian God. Try putting that in a school report.' She giggled, still unable to completely process the events that had taken place. 'We aren't Gods, or superheroes or even adults, but you, me and Stef, we stuck together. We used what we had and we got through it. If we can get through that, we can get through anything.'

'Hey guys, you need to come and look at this,' Stefan's distracted voice beckoned them. Nora and Jacob turned to see Stefan face to face with the Librarian. His nose almost touching hers.

'Stef what are you doing, mate? I hope you're not trying to kiss her. That's just gross!' Jacob laughed. Stef jumped back realising just how close he was to Miss Ali.

'No, don't be stupid. She blinked.'

Jacob and Nora stopped dead in their tracks. 'What do you mean?' Jacob asked, a little spark of hope igniting in his chest. Jumping to their feet they joined him on either side, all staring into the blank eyes of the Priestess.

'Are you sure?' Nora asked sceptically. 'She doesn't look any different.' She secretly hoped she was wrong. They all continued to stare, looking for a sign, a twitch a wink. Any indication she was in there. They needed hope.

They got it.

A blink. Followed by another a few moments later, followed by another until eventually Miss Ali began to stir. Jacob spoke first, 'Is that you Miss?'

The High Priestess raised her hand slowly to her face, turning it round, as if only seeing it for the first time, glancing from her hand to three faces before her, trying to work out if this was real. How was she back?

'Miss, are you okay?' Nora gently pressed. Miss Ali nodded slowly, becoming more aware as her soul settled back in her body. She looked around at the rest of the hall, still frozen around them.

'Children, we need to go, before everyone else returns. There will be fewer questions that way I think.'

Nodding in agreement they gathered the book and the amulets, making a hasty exit from the hall towards the library. As they entered the library, the Priestess scooped the three of them into her arms, engulfing them in an awkward hug. Upon release, they were all blushing, staring at the ground.

'I don't know how you did it, but I am eternally grateful. The Gods are in your debt.'

Nora showed her the two amulets, placing them in her hands. She stared at the undamaged one, holding the God Sett. She could feel the darkness pulsating from it, angry and vengeful.

'I must leave now and return to the Underworld where Sett can be vanquished once and for all. None of the students or teachers will remember anything, so I would suggest this is your little secret,' she said with a wink.

'Who would believe us anyway, Miss?' Jacob said confused. She looked at him with a warm smile.

'I would.'

Taking the book and the amulets, she opened the door once more, entering into the depths of the House of Life, nodding to each of them before closing the heavy door behind her. As the door shut the bookcase slid back into place. As if it had never moved at all.

The three of them took once last glance at the wall and each other before heading down to the hall to check everyone else was ok.

As they approached the hall, Deputy head Miss Cleveland was waiting at the door.

'Come on you three lazy bones or you'll be late for assembly,' she said trying to sound serious, with a soft smile on her face. They glanced between each other before racing into the hall, taking their seats at the back, each with a huge grin on their faces.

Miss Cleveland took to the stage. 'Good Morning and welcome students, to your first day at Nomed Academy. I am Miss Cleveland, your Deputy Head. Unfortunately, your Headmaster, Mr Siriso, couldn't be with us this morning but I hope you'll make do with me for now instead.'

Nora, Stef and Jacob exchanged a knowing glance, before continuing to listen to the Deputy.

'Here at Nomed Academy, we hope to help each of you succeed. You each have choices to make and we want to help you make the wisest of choices to lead you down the right path.'

94

Deja vu hit the trio. They were sure that sounded familiar. Miss Cleveland continued.

'School is an adventure you will never forget, and there will be many tasks along the way, but we as a school are here to guide you along that path and help you conquer those challenges. Together as a team. Welcome to Nomed and enjoy your adventures.'

She stepped down leaving another teacher to hand out announcements as their minds wandered over what she had said. She didn't know, did she? There was no way she could? She walked passed the three of them and out of the hall with a smile they couldn't quite place.

It just couldn't be.

Chapter Sixteen

Term continued on, thankfully quite quietly. School was dull and boring and the trio couldn't have been more grateful for the normality of everyday school life.

Headmaster Siriso retired due to ill health, according to the announcement that followed a week into school. Rumours flew round the Academy ranging from stories that he had run away with the Librarian, to some claiming he'd been sacked and others that he was an ex-convict on the run. Of course Stef, Nora and Jacob knew the truth, but they had sworn to each other never to speak a word of what happened, to anyone. Not that anyone would have believed them anyway.

A new Head was due to start at the end of term and until then, Miss Cleveland was in charge, which made a nice change from Headmaster Siriso. She could usually be found in the library if anyone was looking for her.

It had also become a favourite place for the trio to hang out as well. They felt a special connection to it after everything that happened there. They even tried every book on the shelf to see if they could find the door again, but they couldn't find the one to move the bookcase.

'You three in here again? I'm not sure who spends more time here - you or me?' Miss Cleveland chuckled, as she rearranged the books. She wasn't sure why but she was drawn to the library as well, and after the old Librarian had just upped and left, she had adopted it, looking after it in her free time. It was much less dusty now, with slightly less Egyptian books. How anyone would want to leave the place she couldn't fathom.

'Just doing homework Miss Cleveland, it's nice and quiet in here,' Nora offered as a reply. The Deputy nodded, continuing to sort through the books. It was the last day of term and she wanted everything organised for when the new head arrived. She didn't even have a name or a date when they were arriving which made it harder to prepare. The children were sure she knew more than she was letting on, but how could they prove it? None of them was prepared to ask her about it, in case they were wrong or she just denied it.

97

It was their last day together before returning home for the holidays and the three of them were nervous about being apart for the first time since it had all started. Nobody could understand how such different children could have become such close friends. Their response was always the same.

'We met when we were running late to assembly and we just kind of clicked. The rest, as they say, is history.'

As they giggled quietly in the corner of the library, the door creaked open as the echo of footsteps crossed the floor.

Nobody ever visited the library at this time of day; they were too busy enjoying their free time.

An expensive looking pair of black heels delicately strolled across the library floor clicking with each step, to where Miss Cleveland was arranging the books.

'Ah you must be Miss Cleveland. Delightful. I am your new Head Mistress Pandora Sekhmet.' She smiled, shaking the bewildered Deputy's hand with her tanned, toned skin and flawlessly manicured nails shimmering in the light. Miss Cleveland looked suspiciously at the woman before her before shaking herself.

'A pleasure to meet you, Miss Sekhmet. let me show you to your office.'

She glanced to the table where the students were sitting in stunned silence, mouths gaping open like fish out of water.

'I'll be right back children. I'm just going to show our new Headmistress up to her office.'

She followed the immaculately dressed Headmistress out of the library smiling reassuringly at the children before she left. They weren't reassured. They were frozen in shock, unable to speak or move.

100

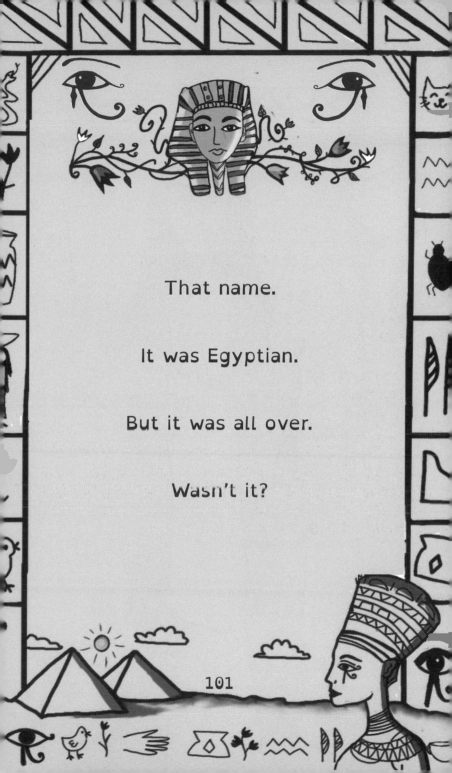

That name.

It was Egyptian.

But it was all over.

Wasn't it?

NOMED

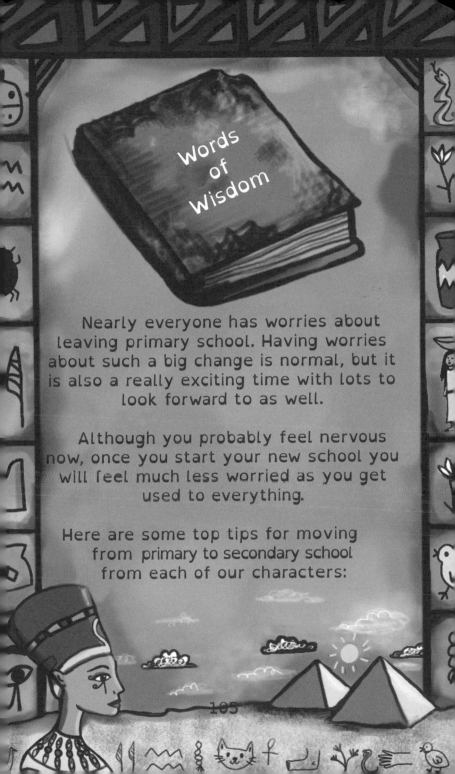

Words
of
Wisdom

Nearly everyone has worries about leaving primary school. Having worries about such a big change is normal, but it is also a really exciting time with lots to look forward to as well.

Although you probably feel nervous now, once you start your new school you will feel much less worried as you get used to everything.

Here are some top tips for moving from primary to secondary school from each of our characters:

It's good to talk

Hi i'm Jacob.

I'm quiet and I often keep my worries to myself, this has made me feel lonely at times and I can find it difficult to concentrate at school.

I felt so relieved when Stef and Nora encouraged me to talk about my worries.

Sharing our feelings can make us feel less worried and remember,
lots of people feel like you do!
Talk to someone you trust.

Try something new

Hi i'm Eleanora,
but you can call me Nora.

I am not adventurous or brave but
I was determined to succeed in my
mission. I was the first one to step
forward and enter the unknown,
and it all worked out well
in the end.

Secondary school is full of
opportunities to try something
new. You may even find your
hidden talent and make some new
friends along the way!

Find out about all the extra clubs
and fun activities you can be
involved in at lunchtime or after
school.

Be yourself

Hi I'm Stefan,
my friends just call me Stef.

Jacob, Nora and I are all very different
to each other. We all have different
personalities and come from different
places. I must admit I felt quite
nervous when I first met them,
even if I didn't show it.

I found it easier to make friends with
them by being myself and cracking
lots of jokes!

Being kind, asking questions and
listening to others all help when
meeting new people.

Practise and prepare

Hello there, I'm Miss Ali, High Priestess
and keeper of the books
in the House of Life.

I had been trapped in the library for as
long as I can remember, so I had plenty of
time to practise and prepare my escape!

We feel more relaxed when we are well
prepared. You can use the summer
holiday to do your research ready for
secondary school and practise your new
route to school. Try packing your bag the
night before and make sure your uniform
is ready and you have time for breakfast
on your first day.

So ... How did Stef, Nora and Jacob
defeat an Egyptian God?
It was not magic or strength. No,
it was fact wise choices, teamwork and
positive thinking!

Secondary school may seem daunting and
will be full of challenges and new
experiences, but take each day one at a
time and always try your best.

Curse of the Nomed
By B B Taylor and Holly Bushnell

Copyright 2018 © Wesleyan

www.curseofthenomed.co.uk

This book was written in the
Spring of 2018 and the story was
created in partnership with pupils
from Four Dwellings Academy.

The themes in the story were inspired by the real
life experiences of the pupils when they
started secondary school.

All net profit from the sales of this book will be
donated to Partnership for Children to continue their
schools based programmes to give
primary school children good mental health for life.
www.partnershipforchildren.org.uk

PARTNERSHIP FOR
Children
Good mental health for children - for life

The full cost of producing this book has been
funded by Wesleyan
www.wesleyan.co.uk/cr

WESLEYAN

we are all about you